~

Furthermore, the Lake

~

1366B99ks

Ontario

Canadä

ONTARIO ARTS COUNCIL
CONSEIL DES ARTS DE L'ONTARIO

an Ontario government agency
un organisme du gouvernement de l'Ontario

Canada Council   Conseil des arts
for the Arts   du Canada

~

Furthermore, the Lake

~

~

Michael e. Casteels

1366Books

Guernica founder: Antonio D'Alfonso
General editor: Michael Mirolla
1366 Books editor: Stuart Ross
Interior design & typesetting: Stuart Ross
Cover & 1366 logo design: Underline Studio
Author photo: Bryan Greer

Guernica Editions Inc.
1241 Marble Rock Rd., Gananoque, ON K7G 2V4
2250 Military Road, Tonawanda, NY 14150-6000 USA
www.guernicaeditions.com

Distributors:
Independent Publishers Group (IPG), 600 North Pulaski Rd., Chicago IL 60624
University of Toronto Press Distribution (UTP), 5201 Dufferin St., Toronto Ontario M3H 5T8

First edition. Printed in Canada.

Library of Congress Control Number: 2024951683

Library and Archives Canada Cataloguing in Publication
Title: Furthermore, the lake / Michael e. Casteels.
Names: Casteels, Michael E., 1985- author.
Description: Series statement: 1366 books ; 3
Identifiers: Canadiana (print) 20240535367 | Canadiana (ebook) 20240537688 | ISBN
9781771839976
(softcover) | ISBN 9781771839983 (EPUB)
Subjects: LCGFT: Novels.
Classification: LCC PS8605.A8745 F87 2025 | DDC C813/.6—dc23

for you, you,
you, and you

•••

Before the beginning, there was brick. Before you. Before me. Before a hand to place the brick alone in a fallow field. Before loon calls and cemeteries, phone calls and forgetting. Before the subway. Before the doors. Before fog and boxes, toothbrushes and blue. Before rain, ghosts, and the lake. Before the red canoe. Before the night that stretched forever into the end, and long before the before, was the brick, waiting, waiting to begin.

~

Decapitated sparrow. Vivisected mouse. Star-nosed mole with a broken neck. Every morning I'd discover the latest victim, tortured and slain on my welcome mat. A disembowelled rat or a robin with wrenched wings. I dumped the bodies in my compost bin, didn't know what else to do. If I buried them I'd become caretaker to a miniature cemetery in my backyard. A perpetual mourner. My wardrobe would be exclusively black. I'd shuffle through rows of popsicle-stick crosses, laying dandelions on graves, humming hymns, wailing laments.

The perpetrator's identity was a mystery to me. The orange tabby across the road? The calico next door? The black cat with white paws or the striped one with a tattered ear? My garden was their litter box. My lawn furniture, their scratching posts. Their yowls invaded my dreams and woke me to cold sweats.

It could have been any one of them.

Eviscerated rabbit. Loose tail of a squirrel. Chipmunk with rigor mortis. I couldn't take it anymore, the plethora of gruesome gifts, and I resolved to confront the murderer, face to face. I brewed an evening coffee and sat by the window, peeking through the crack where the curtains didn't quite meet.

A night can drag its feet when it wants to, and that night it wanted to. The occasional car. An infrequent passerby. But when the late hours finally shifted into the early hours, even these ceased. The street lights shone down on nothing but cracks in the pavement. There wasn't a moth to speak of. But I stayed attentive, a solitary sentinel, scanning my vacant front step, the empty sidewalk, and the street where a thin wisp of fog slowly rolled in. It grew thick and dense, quietening the night further toward silence, obscuring my view. I couldn't even see the street.

I opened my door and stepped into this blurred world. The fog enveloped me. I breathed in its damp asphalt smell, its hint of rain. The fog flowed into my lungs and drifted into my head, where my thoughts came unmoored and drifted off. I was lost in the fog between these thoughts, the thought of which drifted off in the fog, leaving me alone in the fog with a pile of feathers at my feet.

~

The subway station, flooded with commuters. I'd just finished work, and along with the rest of this bustling city I was carried in the current, like a cell of some enormous organism, uncertain of the role it played in the existence of the whole. The drone of our footfalls filled the long corridors. The odd voice rose above the undertone. We pressed shoulder to shoulder, alone within ourselves, standing on the platform now, waiting for the rush of air that meant our deliverance was near.

Seated. Squeezed between strangers. The subway car swayed, the monotonous clicking of its wheels lulled us. A few people spoke in hushed voices, not wanting to disturb the silence of their loner companions-in-travel. I glanced up at the advertisements lining the wall of the car: an attractive couple with bright smiles, each showing off a brand-new toothbrush; a lakeside vacation destination, golden sand and crashing waves; a man looking out a subway window, catching his reflection in the glass—the words above his head read *You are Who?* I didn't know what it was selling. I looked out the window, caught my reflection looking back, likely reflecting on that very same question.

The doors hissed closed behind me and the train whooshed off, stirring scraps of paper that littered the ground. My footsteps echoed through this now quiet space. I walked to the escalator, and as I rose I heard faint music that grew steadily louder. When I reached the next floor, you came into view from above: dressed in white and playing a large wooden harp.

The tune was slow, mournful, and had been playing for all time. Each note weighed in the air like a resonant fog. My pace slowed with every step, as if you or the harp were the source of an intense gravitational pull, where time slowed and nearly ceased. I neared. I nearly ceased. Your head low, eyes closed, fingers gliding over strings that heaved like waves. My legs were heavy. The light was dim. A thousand years passed as I fished through my pockets, found a single coin, and dropped it into your empty hat.

~

The further I walked, the closer I got. To what, I wasn't sure, but my feet kept moving, carrying the rest of me along with them. They had their own preconceived destination—somewhere they might finally settle down, a little slice of heaven, a place to call home. I was just their solitary witness, a quiet companion, the documenter of their long journey.

It was easy. They walked; I followed.

The path snaked along the lakeside. The sky was a dark canvas the stars punched small holes into one by one. A sickle moon crept up from behind the horizon. A large bird beat its enormous wings, faded into distance. Somewhere a duck quacked, then hushed, and the relative silence resumed.

A few soft waves lapped against the shore with a steady rhythm. The small stones cascading across one another clattered out a soft melody. It was a lullaby, though I wasn't sure who was being lulled: me, the city, or the lake itself.

The lake sighed. I sighed.

The city drifted off into the night, far above the lake and me.

~

How long had your leaving resided inside you? Looking back, I'll never know. Your eyes were blue, but what shade? You opened your mouth. A cloud emerged, but what shape? Looking back, I'll never know. The photographs and memories, gnawed by time. What time is it where you are now? Here it keeps changing. Just when I've got it figured out, it's another day, another season.

~

The muffin or the scone, I can't decide but I must, and soon, the customers lined up behind me are tapping feet, clearing throats, twisting to peer over my shoulder at the options, a muffin or scone, and the barista waits expectantly with tongs in her hand and a hand on her hip, and it's not as easy as everyone thinks, this multiple choice exam, this pressure building like steam, and I haven't even considered coffee, the size or the roast or the number of shots, the milk or the cream or the dairy-free options, the sugars and syrups and infinite flavours, and another impatient sigh, the line straining and the whole café silent and staring, and it's enough to tear me in two, each half going their own way with a different pastry in hand, and it's enough to splinter each me even further when asked, morning glory or chocolate chip, or cheddar or blueberry, butter or margarine, and I'm in six different places and each choice fractions me further and further toward some distant decimal place where everywhere I look, there I am with every possible coffee and every possible pastry and the café has never done better business, but the line is impossibly long, stretching out the door, and I must decide, the muffin or the scone, and to which universe I'll belong when I finally place my order.

~

The officer taps on my window with his flashlight. I roll it down. "Good evening, sir," he says. "Have you been drinking?"

"No," I reply, because I haven't. He asks if I know how fast I was going, and I say, "One-twenty."

He says, "One twenty-eight." And I say, "I'm sorry sir."

The officer taps on my window with his flashlight. I roll it down. He yanks his gun from its holster, points it at my head, says, "Get the hell out of your car and get your hands on your head, or I swear to god, I'll shoot you down in ten, nine, eight..." I struggle with my seatbelt. It won't come undone.

The officer taps on my window with his flashlight. I roll it down. He has the face of a fish, his eyes glazed, his mouth puckered like he's gasping for air. I tell him to get in. I tear down the highway, turn at the old stone bridge, skid into the gravel parking lot. I carry the officer down to the shore, slip him into the river.

The officer taps on my window with his flashlight. I tap back with mine.

The officer taps on my window with his flashlight, and I know, after all these years, they've finally caught up with me. I reach down, into that pocket in the driver's side door...

The officer taps on my window with his flashlight, and I say, "What's this about?" He says, "You were speeding." I say, "This is my *house*," and he looks around, nodding and muttering, "Oh yes, houses are the stationary ones."

The officer taps his flashlight. It won't turn on. He's alone on a dark highway. The night is still. A nearby bush rustles.

~

The email came down from management: Staff Party. Conference Room. 5 p.m. No indication of what we were celebrating. It wasn't a holiday. There'd been no increase in sales. No retirements or promotions. A party for the sake of a party?

At the end of my shift, I left my office and headed toward the conference room. A table had been set up along the far wall with a bowl of red punch, a platter with tiny triangular sandwiches, a bag of plain chips.

A few of my co-workers were already there. John from accounting was loosening his tie and taking a quick swig from a flask. Yoko from HR was sipping a glass of punch, half-listening to Laura who was gulping it down and starting to slur, like maybe it had been spiked.

Omar from IT wheeled in a dusty old television. "I just found this in the utility room. Let's see if I can set it up—there's a box of VHS we could break into."

Margery was still at her desk, calculating the week's profits and losses. Jim walked in, headed straight for the chips, and started snacking. Nadia sat in the corner, staring down at her cellphone. She looked up at me: "Any idea how long this party will be? I want to get home before my kids go to bed."

"No idea," I said. And really, none of us knew how long it would last. Management never said, and they hadn't arrived yet. We'd become prisoners to the whole debacle. Hanging out at work, chatting about work, while the world outside moved on, forgetting us moment by moment.

~

I heard it through the graveyard. You didn't make it. Everyone else was there. Late fall, dusk arriving early. The sky was headstone grey. Long grass swayed in stray gusts of wind. The leafless branches of a nearby oak creaked like wooden bones. A quiet crow on a bare limb. With one hand, I held my hat tight to my head. I gripped my umbrella in the other. Voices spoke and I was there, but hardly. I remember a hymn, but not which one. I remember my mother's long overcoat, my father's reddened eyes. The pile of dirt draped with Astroturf. The rectangular hole, an emptiness longing to be filled. The heavy air trembled with distant thunder. We'd just begun as the first drops fell. Umbrellas bloomed like black roses. A prayer I don't remember. Faces downturned. The rain repeating our every word.

~

The bathtub is running and I'm trying to keep up. Its four clawed feet sprint across the pavement, clack clack, clack clack, clack clack. Its water sloshes and spills into the street, but the rain pours down, filling it again.

My feet are bare. My towel is soaked. My hair, still full of suds.

Here's what happened: I got home late. I was beat. I didn't want to think about a thing. I headed for the bathroom, popped the plug into the drain, cranked the hot water tap. I grabbed a fresh towel, undressed, and waited.

When the tub was full, I slipped into the steaming water, let out a sigh, and submerged my head. The day's tension seeped out of my body; this was just what I needed. I surfaced, squirted shampoo into my hands, and lathered my hair. Then the phone started ringing. I just let it ring. Whoever it was could wait until tomorrow. But the ringing didn't stop. Two minutes was all I could take. I climbed out of the tub, grabbed my towel, and stomped out of the washroom. I snatched up the phone and nearly shouted, "Hello?"

The bathtub is surprisingly agile for its age. You'd think it would lumber like a hippopotamus, but it's more like a rhinoceros charging blindly into the night. I'm a few hundred metres behind it and losing ground. The bathtub leaps over a white picket fence, rounds a corner, and then it's gone.

There was no answer on the other end. I said it again, more agitated: "Hello? Anyone there? Don't you know what time it is?" I listened closer. It wasn't just dead air. I heard someone breathing. "Hello? Who the hell is this?" Still no reply, just faint breath coming down the line. I was losing steam. "Is everything all right? Can I help? Please, talk to me. I'm sorry, I don't know what else to say..."

The rain stings my bare chest. My feet are cold, standing in a puddle in the street. And no, I'm not crying, it's just the rain getting shampoo in my eyes.

•••

Beside the brick a brick is born, and beside this, a brick. A brick is born on top of a brick, beside which a brick is born. Atop these, a brick, and beside this brick, a brick. And with its foundation begun, the building is born.

~

Fog is what I remember. Fog and little else. Vague forms. Splotches of shadow in the grey. All fine detail, a haze. I picked up my phone but couldn't see the numbers. I opened a book but couldn't read a word. When I looked in the mirror, I was a blob looking back. The days took on this opaque quality: faint light, false dusk, all stretching into one day that didn't end. The clock on the wall ticked but I couldn't read the time. I slept but woke fitful, uncertain how long I'd been out. I'd shuffle to the front door, throw it open, hopeful the sky would be blue. But it was always the same grey. The sun lost somewhere in it. I'd look out to the street but couldn't see the sidewalk. If I left, I'd never make it back home. I felt a thousand kilometres away from everything. My house, adrift at sea.

~

I was swimming in the sea and something brushed against my legs. No. That wasn't it. I was swimming in the lake and the waves, capped with white foam, pushed me under. But that's only part of it. A current tugged me out into deep water. I kicked and paddled frantically, but every time I looked, the shore was further away. You stood there, feet in the sand, hands cupped around your mouth, hollering, "You okay?"

"Yes!" I shouted, though I certainly wasn't. My arms and legs were tiring. My lungs burned. I didn't know how much longer I could tread. A wave shoved me under and drew me out further.

I surfaced, coughing and choking. Searching for you, I noticed a cluster of rocks rising out of the water. They were halfway between me and the shore, offering a possible reprieve to catch my breath. A wave collapsed over me. I turned toward the rocks and swam hard. A wave pushed me under. The outcrop edged closer. A wave crashed, I swallowed water, kept paddling. When one of the rocks was finally within reach, an unruly wave lifted me and tumbled me over it, nearly bashing my skull. I realized then the danger I'd put myself in. A wave tackled me, threw me against another rock. In the brief lull of the wave's retreat I grabbed onto the rock, but my grip was weak and a wave tore me off, tugged me down. I broke the surface, gasping. In the next lull I found a decent handhold. A wave rushed over me, and I felt my grip loosening. I hauled myself up, got my feet beneath me, and before another wave could crash, I leapt off, toward the shore.

The heavy waves grasped at my legs, but I was out of the undertow and making headway through the surf. When my feet touched sand, I knew I'd be okay. I walked out of the water and collapsed, my limbs trembling. The clouds gazed down in their mad rush across the sky. The sun glared into my eyes, until you, a silhouette, stood above me and said, "Are you sure you're okay?"

All I could say was, "Yup."

~

I remember a canoe in the lake, a red canoe, but no one in it. I remember the lake welling inside me. I remember my eyes brimming. I remember the phone ringing, saying, "Hello, Blue." My eyes brimming. I remember a voice entering one ear and sneaking out through a crack in my pericardium. I remember picking up a brick and hucking it into the lake. I remember the lake hucking it back, the brick landing at my feet, a note tied to it with white string. The blue ink was smeared, but I could still make out the words *Hello, Blue*.

~

I remember your hand resting on my stomach. Or was it my hand on yours? We were on the bed, watching the ceiling fan rotate. Or we were on the couch, watching a late-night talk show. Your hand on my stomach, gliding up and down, or my hand on yours, tracing slow circles. With tears in your eyes, you leaned into my shoulder. Or my cheeks were wet, and you dried them with your sleeve. The window was closed, curtains drawn. We were sealed from the outside world. Or the window was open, and our lives made an escape. The words we said. The words we hadn't.

I turned to face you, or you turned your face to me, and a strand of hair stuck to your cheek. I brushed it away. A strand of hair stuck to your cheek. I brushed it away. A strand of hair stuck to your cheek. I brushed it away. A strand of hair stuck to your cheek. I brushed it away. You said something then, but it's different every time.

You said, "Can nothing change your mind?" You said, "Nothing can change my mind." You said, "I won't be gone long." You said, "I'll be long gone." You said, "I love you." You said, "I loved you."

~

The day had grown old. I watched the sun's last rays dip beneath the horizon. For a while I sat there, in the faint glow that remained. The fire crackled yellow and orange as it spread through the kindling. I placed a few larger sticks and, once those caught, a decent-sized log. The lake lay quiet, reflective. A stray cloud stared back at itself.

Far out on the lake a loon released a soft warble, and before it could finish, another took up the call, wailing. A third and fourth responded, with trills and hoots and ululations. Then, just as quickly, the lake quieted. Cricket chirp. Frog croak. Branch creak.

For a while nothing much happened, which happened to be the point of it all. The log caught fire, and I added another. The cloud moved along, revealing a single star and its reflection. A loon called. Another's response. A few sparks flickered upward, mingling with the fireflies lingering in the gathering dusk.

~

A memory just came to me. It was mid-summer, early August. I was eleven or twelve and working for a farmer down the road, helping bring in the hay. I walked through the fresh-cut fields, and the farmer drove alongside me in his truck. We stopped every few metres, where the bales were gathered, and we piled them into the pickup. The work was dry and itchy, and the sun was working as hard as me. I'd brought a jug full of ice water. It was empty by noon.

Later we were in the hayloft making space, moving piles of dusty cardboard boxes. I picked one up and was startled by something bright and squirming beneath it. It took a moment for me to recognize—a nest of baby mice, furless and pink, all snuggled together. I looked around, wondering where I should move them, to keep them safe. I was about to ask, when the farmer approached and saw what I was looking at. Without a pause he stepped forward and began stomping. I'd never seen anything like it. The loose hay coming up with his boot. The dull thud of impact. Then he picked up the last box and carried it out of the barn without saying a word.

I remember his farm. I passed it every day on my way to school. I remember the exact blue of the sky. I remember the low stubble in the field. I remember the proper way to stack hay, so the piles are steady and there's no risk of tipping. I remember the way my shoulders ached. I remember the farmer's face; his expression never changed. But I don't remember his name. I only met him that once.

~

Inside the cardboard box I find a view overlooking the lake, a lone seagull wheeling in the wind. The wind came from a box labelled *Wind*. The lake fills a box labelled *Lake*. I open a box labelled *Sky*, find a cloud stuffed at the bottom. I pick it up, shake it out, and wait while it slowly inflates. Inside the cloud is a box labelled *Rain*; it leaks. The lake is pocked by raindrops. The wind blows the rain right into my face. I close the box with a view of the lake and turn to a box labelled *Fragile: Handle with Care*. I open this box, but it's empty. I crawl inside and close the flaps. Someone was kind enough to poke holes in the lid. I look up into my little bit of sky. The stars all squint back at me.

•••

Walls arise. A staircase ascends one step at a time. A ceiling caps the walls, and above it a floor lies down as the walls continue upward and the staircase climbs higher and another ceiling becomes the next floor. The windows, no longer ground-level, gaze out over the field and witness the birth of scattered bricks beside which bricks are born, and the city begins to crawl.

~

You left, but your toothbrush remains. Black handle. White neck. Worn bristles. Standing in the cup next to mine. When I enter the bathroom, my eyes gravitate toward it and my memories gravitate to you: brushing, gargling, rinsing, spitting, and finally, your smile, flashing back from deep within the mirror.

There's nothing else. Your bags carried the rest of you away. Your shoes followed you out the door. I asked why, but your response was the creaking door, the jingle of keys, the engine turning over, and finally, the silence of taillights shrinking into the dark.

Your toothbrush remains, and mine stands beside it. They face one another. I lean them closer. Their bristles entwine, and I turn away, glimpsing my reflection.

My reflection thinks I need a shave and to get some sun. It worries about me. But me, I'm worried about your teeth, now that your toothbrush has decided to stay. I worry about your smile, flashing back at you from some other mirror.

I squirt a little toothpaste onto my brush, but the tube is thin. I've rolled it from the bottom up, been nursing it for weeks. There's only enough left for one. Even my reflection will have to wait.

~

Another memory just came to me. I was younger, maybe seven or eight. The game was hide-and-seek, but Grandpa didn't know the rules.

"It's easy," I said, "you hide, I'll seek." I closed my eyes and counted to one hundred. I wanted to give him a chance, he was so slow he could hardly climb the stairs into the house. "Ready or not, here I come!" I yelled. Even with the extra time he wouldn't have made it very far. I checked the obvious spots—behind the living room curtains, inside the coat closet, in the bathtub, but he wasn't there. I checked beneath my bed, behind the couch. I had no idea where he was. I scoured each room, examined impossible spots— under my father's desk, inside kitchen cupboards, I even opened the fridge. "Grandpa!" I finally yelled. "It's time to come out. You win!" I waited and he didn't appear. I wondered about his hearing aids—had the battery died? If so, he'd never hear me. He'd never know when to come out of hiding. I worked my way through the rooms methodically. I moved every object I could. I tore each room apart.

When Mom got home that night she was livid.

"What did you do the house?" she cried.

"It's Grandpa," I said, "I lost him." Her expression suddenly softened from anger to concern. She lifted me into her arms and carried me upstairs to my room, where she kissed me on the forehead and tucked me into bed.

I couldn't sleep, though it was well past my bedtime. I listened to my mother downstairs, walking from room to room, opening cupboards I couldn't reach and investigating all the other spots I'd likely missed.

~

I wake up but feel exhausted. I wake up and I'm ready to hit the hay. I wake up and suddenly the day's begun. This is how I wake ninety percent of the time, my battery at ten percent, still in need of a charge. I'm falling and the morning rushes up to greet me. I'm never prepared. I close my eyes and my eyes snap open and I'm another day older. My alarm clock stares at me. I wake up reading where I left off. I wake fully dressed, my shoes already tied, briefcase in hand, and I'm heading out the door. I wake when the dump truck rattles my bedroom window, when the robin loses its head, when my alarm clock tells me to.

I should have closed the curtains because now the sun's come waltzing in, and there's no sweeping it away. I wake sweeping. I wake weeping. I wake too early, close my eyes and wake up later, when the world is ready for me. I close my eyes and miss my cue. I wake and the moon is peeking into my sock drawer. I close my eyes and wake up broken, then close my eyes, and wake up repaired but with aftermarket parts and dodgy wiring. I'd wake, but I'm awake. I'd fall asleep, but the day is tapping its foot. When I wake I'm a new person, though I'm exactly the same as before. I fall asleep to my eyes opening every time I close my eyes.

~

The first time I ran away from home, I stuffed my backpack with clothes and tucked an old sleeping bag beneath my arm. I'd scrounged all my loose change and dumped it into a sock. The general store was within walking distance, and they sold five-cent candies, so I figured my money would last a few days. I walked down the stairs and through the kitchen, where my mother sat at the kitchen table, plucking her eyebrows.

"Where are you off to?"

"I'm running away."

"Oh, okay," she replied, looking into the little free-standing mirror on the table in front of her. "Just be home before dark."

I headed toward the forest that bordered our property, passed through some thick underbrush, and then I was alone. When I turned around I couldn't see the house. Those woods were my familiar playground, but that day they felt foreign, like if I went too far I might never find my way back. I gripped my sleeping bag and headed on.

I remember the yellow-orange light sifting down through the canopy. I remember the moist smell of decomposition. The air was cool but not cold, and I trekked through a dense thicket of pine, around a stagnant beaver pond, beneath a towering oak tree hundreds of years old, further than I'd ever gone before.

A while later I came to a cedar rail fence. I climbed over it into a long pasture where a tall chestnut horse lifted its head from grazing and stared at me. I noted a small lean-to tucked into a grove of trees and headed toward it. As I walked, the horse's head turned to follow me.

The lean-to was just plywood on three walls and a sheet-metal roof on top, a place for the horse to keep out of the rain. Inside was neat enough. There were some scattered flakes of hay and a few mounds of horse droppings, but I shovelled those out with a pitchfork I found on the wall. I set my backpack down in a corner where the dirt was undisturbed. I unrolled my sleeping bag and crawled inside. I'd done it. I'd run away from home.

But as I lay there, I couldn't remember what I was running from, or where I was running to, or what set my feet in motion that morning. I sat up and looked out the doorway. The horse was walking toward me. I got up and stepped out to greet it. The horse towered over me as it approached, and I offered my open hands for it to smell. Its velvety nose pressed into my palms, enormous nostrils flaring. I stood to one side, stroking its broad neck and speaking softly. Its ears twitched and twisted with every word. When the horse looked down at me, its eye was a dark horizon in a gaseous cloud of stars. I felt drawn into that oblique galaxy, worlds away from the life I'd been running from. I stood on a vast and open prairie, a herd of wild horses thundering over the undulated landscape, manes and tails like waves of variegated light, flowing into and out of one another, until, in the midst of the dust that lifted into the air, they became one horse, one I could ride like a cowboy into the sunset, but this horse, the father of all horses, could take me into the sun itself, and beyond that, to some unknowable distance where I'd finally dismount into the life that had been waiting for me.

But after a minute the horse turned and headed back out to the field. Its tail swished, flicking away the few late-season flies that drifted in the waning afternoon sunlight.

~

Just then, the phone rang. I picked up the receiver and said, "Hello?"

"Hello, Mr. MacIntosh."

"Sorry, you've got the wrong number."

"This is the number we've got on file."

"I'm the only one here, and I'm not Mr. MacIntosh."

"Do you know when he'll be in?"

"No, I mean he doesn't live here."

"Do you know what number we can reach him at?"

"I've never met the guy. I have no idea who he is."

"In that case, would you care to answer a few questions regarding the quality of service you received last week."

"I didn't receive any service last week. I don't think I'll be much help."

"Let me be the judge of that. Here's the first question. On a scale of one to five, one being the least likely and five the most likely, how would you recommend our service to your friends or family?"

"I don't even know what kind of service you provide."

"That's not a number, sir. I need a number."

"Well, zero then. I wouldn't recommend it to anyone."

"Zero isn't on the scale, sir. But I'll mark it as a one. Here's your second question. Using the same scale, how satisfied are you with our service?"

"Uh. One, I guess."

"What could we have done better? What would you like to see changed in our service?"

"This is getting ridiculous. I think I'm finished here."

"I just have one more question. Please stay on the line—if you hang up now, it'll throw off my service stats for the day. If you were given the choice between the life you're currently living or the life of someone else, entirely at random, what would you choose?"

"Well...sometimes I get this feeling that I was born five minutes too early, or five minutes too late, in the wrong hospital, in the wrong town, on the wrong side of the world, on the wrong planet, and now I'm stumbling to keep up with a life that is always a few steps ahead of me, or I stare at my watch, waiting for my life to catch up... but I've been in this life for as long as I can remember, it's the only life I've ever known..."

"That's not much of an answer, sir."

"Sorry, sorry. It'll take me some time to think it over."

"Please don't take long. It'll affect my call-time stats. My manager has been hounding me. So what do you think? This life or someone else's?"

"At this moment, I guess I'd take someone else's. But if you asked me five minutes ago, or five minutes from now, I'd probably have kept my own."

"Thank you, Mr. MacIntosh. It's been a pleasure speaking with you. You may receive a follow-up call for the service you've received today. Please give me a positive review, it will help with my stats. And have a pleasant day."

The line went dead. I stood there with the receiver in my hand, wondering about Mr. MacIntosh, and what his answers would have been. I set the phone down, opened the cupboard, looked for something to eat.

~

I told you I'd be there soon, but something came up. You're not going to believe it. I was in the cemetery, digging. I was on the beach building a castle. I was in the forest, trying to find my way home. My watch seized; I tapped its face, but its hands remained motionless. The map I planned to use got buried in sand. I was swimming in the lake, the undertow dragging me further from shore. I couldn't find a street sign. Somehow the doorknob got reversed and I was locked inside my house. Somehow the lights went out. I was only a child. You were too. You're the one who said it. Time doesn't change, everything else does. The refrigerator idled while inside everything decayed, but slowly. I opened the door but couldn't decide. I kept digging. The castle kept growing. Every tree looked exactly the same. I was out of breath but didn't call for help. I stubbed my toe on the coffee table and my life flashed. I was only a child. You were in a nursing home, forgetting me. I was an old man with false teeth. You hadn't been born yet. You glanced in the mirror. I jumped back in shock, but when I looked again it was just me all along. I was in a movie. The scene went like this: The hole was knee-deep, and I jabbed the spade into the earth. A stray cat emerged from the collective dark. The treetops swayed in unison. The officer tapped my window with his flashlight. My car, engulfed in flames. I knew I'd be late. I knew I should call. But I wasn't tall enough to the reach the phone, and you'd been gone for a decade or more. I picked up the phone and said, "Hello, Blue." I searched my pockets and found a hole but not the key. The further I dug, the harder the earth became. I opened the window and looked down at the lake. My hands clawed at the churning waves. The hands on my watch were moving again, but counterclockwise. I told you I'd be there soon, but tomorrow has already passed, and yesterday is just around the corner.

•••

Outward from the building, the city creeps, brick by brick, until the cement trucks emerge from the earth and back into place. The streets are poured. They flow like asphalt rivers around the rising buildings, branching out, sprouting dark street lights. Stop signs bloom on the corners. From the network of waterlines, fire hydrants mushroom to the surface. Bus stops are dropped off at their stops. Benches sit wherever they need a break. A newborn newspaper stand stands upright and steadies itself. The paper costs a quarter. The headline reads, "When the Sun Went Down, All the Lights Turned On."

~

The day the fog lifted, I stepped outside, and the body of a great blue heron lay on the welcome mat, neck twisted, eyes glazed. It was a majestic bird, or at least it had been. Now it was crumpled: enormous wings jutted at unnatural angles, yellow legs splayed like noodles. Its rapier beak was cracked open, tongue dangling. I knelt and cradled its head in my hands. It was only then I noticed: the heron was still breathing.

I looked up and down the street, and every cat was there. The orange tabby, the black cat with two white paws, the striped cat with a tattered ear, the calico, the fat one from three houses down, the long-haired grey, the old tortoiseshell, the two white cats I could never tell apart...and cats I'd never seen before, hundreds, all gathered on the street, their stares fixed on me.

The poor broken bird felt limp in my hands. Its eye fluttered a moment, then went still, and I saw myself reflected, kneeling in its dark pool.

"Oh, Blue," I cried, "not like this. Not again, exactly as before."

~

Getting back to your toothbrush—there's one more thing I want to add. Your toothbrush is so perfectly yours. Its worn bristles are your wispy hair. The way its head angles, it's your head. Even the curves of its handle are your curves. If your toothbrush could speak, it would have your voice, it would remind me to brush, gargle, and floss.

I woke in the night and I swear I heard your toothbrush crying, but when I turned on the bathroom light, it just stood in the cup beside mine, quiet as a toothbrush. I turned off the light and climbed back into bed.

What I'm trying to say is that your toothbrush is still your toothbrush though I'm certain you have another. By now you're likely on your second or third. They never last as long as you think. But this toothbrush will outlive them all. It woke me earlier, but now its silence lulls me back to sleep as the first drops of rain tap against the window. The sky is a leaky faucet about to burst.

~

When the rain began in earnest, I was still in bed. Its beating against the window woke me before my alarm clock had the chance. Six twenty-nine a.m. In one more minute my alarm clock would have rung. I reached over and flicked the switch, then stared up at the ceiling and listened to the rain. The early-morning light was dull and sleepy as it sifted through my curtains. I felt sleepy too. I'd only lost a minute, but felt like I hadn't slept at all.

Waiting for the coffee to brew, I stood at the window, watching the sidewalk puddles grow, and thought about my walk to the subway station. I'd be soaked for sure. The way the rain was coming down, we were clearly in it for the long haul.

This became more apparent once I was out in the downpour. I struggled to keep myself within the safe space beneath my umbrella. Sudden gusts sprayed my face. I lowered my head, trudged on, and though I walked with hurried steps, I managed to avoid the puddles that had become numerous and deep.

When I arrived at the office, a wide puddle had formed in front of the doors. There was no way around it—my feet were going to get wet. I took a tentative step forward and plunged. The water was above my head. I swam to the surface and broke through with a gasp. The rain pelted down. I looked around for a cluster of rocks, but the waves were dark, choppy, and endless in every direction. A streak of lightning split the sky. I clung to my briefcase, which floated like a life preserver.

~

Just then, the phone rang. I picked up the receiver and said, "Hello?"

"How are you feeling today?"

"Who is this?" I asked.

"I'm calling on behalf of a statistics research group. We're doing a survey. Your cooperation would be greatly appreciated. I promise I won't take too much of your time."

"All right," I said. "Ask away."

"I already did. How are you feeling today?"

"Fine."

"I'm sorry, sir, that's not one of the options."

"Good then. I'm good."

"That's not an option either, sir. Please, you need to be completely honest, otherwise the results will be skewed. Try again, and remember your answers will remain anonymous. How are you feeling today?"

I thought for a moment. "Blue," I said. "I'm feeling blue."

"Blue," he said, as if checking off a box on a form. "What shade exactly?"

"What shade?"

"Tuesday-morning blue. Heron blue. Still-lake blue. Mother's-eyes blue. Deoxygenated-blood blue. Forget-me-not blue. Robin's-egg blue. Blue-whale blue..."

"The blue sky. All of it. Looking down at everything else."

"Thank you. Your results have been recorded. Have a pleasant day."

The line went dead and I replaced the receiver in its cradle. My mouth was dry. I opened the cupboard and reached for a glass. I filled the glass with water and gulped it down, then filled it one more time.

~

Earlier I said that when I wake up I'm a new person, even though I'm exactly the same as before, but what I really meant is that when I wake up I could be anyone. I'm anonymous. I walk down the street, take the subway, stop at a favourite café, and no one gives me a second look. I'm a perfect stranger.

Once I reach the office, my co-workers seem to recognize me, but here's the thing: when I walk through the office doors, I leave a portion of myself outside and become someone else entirely. I fume over incorrect photocopies. I rejoice when my pencils are sharpened. I thrill at the crunching of numbers.

But sometimes I stare out the window and wonder what that other part of me is doing. I like to imagine it sits by the door, obediently awaiting my return, but in all likelihood it's in the park, watching the trees sway or the lake ripple. Maybe it feeds pigeons, or chats with strangers on benches. Maybe it's discovered a part of someone else and fallen in love again.

When five o'clock rolls around, I leave the office and that part of me slips back into place, a little altered, a little disappointed. It secretly waits until late at night, when I'm fast asleep, to return to its own life, feeling lighter, without the burden of me weighing it down.

~

Today the lake is smaller than usual. The surface glimmers where the sun beats down. There are no whitecaps, no crashing surf, just the constant undulation of blue.

A new island floats alone in the middle of the lake—rock face, scrub cedar, white pine—like the lake thought it into being overnight, a thought bubble turned Canadian Shield. Today the lake thinks of a seagull flying against the wind, momentarily lost in the white haze of sky. The seagull thinks of two loons. One loon thinks fish flickering like silver in the glare of sunlight. The other loon thinks of me, standing at the edge of the lake.

This is what it means to be thought of by a loon: I'm standing at the edge of the lake, thinking about you. Here I am, and there you are, wherever you are. I'd hoped to be thinking grander thoughts, like the lake, wondering how it got here, at the edge of me. But I'm thinking of you, realizing the lake is in your head too, and I'm the one who put it there.

~

Tonight an empty bag of potato chips scared the hell out of me. I was walking home from the convenience store when the breeze suddenly shifted direction, sending this empty bag of chips skittering across the sidewalk in front of me. I didn't scream, but I did gasp as I flinched and cringed backwards, lifting my foot, like the empty bag of potato chips would scurry up my leg. Normally, I wouldn't be so affected by an empty bag of potato chips, but my mind was still lakeside, and the empty bag of chips lurking in the shadows got the drop on me.

~

You left, and I am sole heir to our memories. Boxes stack toward the ceiling. They fill every space. I can't locate the door or open a window, or find the phone to call you and ask for help. I blow some dust off a box and open it.

I carried you in my arms and twirled you around until you were dizzy. You towered over me and placed your heavy, weathered hand on my shoulder. We walked our bikes up a steep hill. You smiled at me in the mirror, and my reflection smiled back. I held you in my hands, you were that small. I stood on your fingertip and waved. I was microscopic.

A black butterfly lands on my fingertip, its inked wings like a Rorschach test. Then it flits away, carrying my answer before I even know what it is.

The heavy air swallowed all sound, and dark clouds scrolled across the sky, predicting a dreary rain or an isolated shower on this hillside overlooking the quiet hamlet and, furthermore, the lake.

The long line of cars, a hushed parade.

I'm afraid to vacuum. A few of your stray hairs remain, but even these are falling apart, feeding the dust mites and their offspring.

Half a shrew. A house sparrow's head. Vole frozen in eternal panic.

I remember the sky was blue. I was swimming in the lake. The current tugged me outward. The sun on my skin. That's what I remember most.

Not with a bang but a whimper, that's how the world ends. I keep whimpering and the world keeps banging, so I guess we're doing okay for now, though here, in the wilderness, I hear only my whimpers and a black fly buzzing around my ear.

Every wavelet that laps the shore is the lake speaking its thoughts: *invisible tongue, blue sigh, glass tulip, sunken sunlight, shuffled rainclouds, ponderous ellipses of self-doubt...*

The lake remembers a seagull, but it's nowhere to be seen. It remembers loons, but they're gone too. No, wait. I just heard one. A heart-wrenched wail. No response.

This could have been years ago. Or sometime last week. Or three days from now. It's the type of thing that happens again and again, and once started, can't be stopped. A strand of hair stuck to your cheek. I brushed it away. It's the only thing that keeps me from wandering off course. It's what passes through my mind every time I squirt a little toothpaste on my toothbrush.

My eyelids flutter. I wake. My alarm clock is staring at me.

The problem with memory is that it's all about perspective. For example: What I remember, with some certainty, is that we talked all afternoon, but the conversation is hazy. It seemed we'd never be free of the humidity.

I open a box labelled *Little Bits of Sky That Need Gluing*. Inside I find a meteor shooting across a broken piece of atmosphere.

If your toothbrush could speak, I'd speak back, but your toothbrush doesn't have ears and can't hear a thing.

Suddenly, a loud crash outside. I bolted upright, rolled out of bed, and sped to the window. I couldn't see anything, so I ran downstairs, flipped on the lights, and stepped out. The air was humid, the night still. It felt like the rain would start at any second. My garbage can was knocked over. A portly raccoon waddled into darkness.

The midnight lake dips a pen into its black ink and jots down brief thoughts: *horse constellation, laminated moonlight, the frog's music box...*

My hands had traded places. I didn't know what-handed I was anymore. I fumbled everything. Everyone at the office noticed, but no one said a thing.

I open a box labelled *Fragile: Handle with Care*. It's full of shadows, folded neatly and tucked away. I ignore this box and reach for another.

I woke in a hospital. A nurse handed me a clipboard and pushed me through a set of doors into a small room with bright lights. You were lying on the table in front of me, your chest wide open. I didn't want to look, but I did, and I saw your heart. It was my alarm clock, staring at me.

I woke with a nurse above me, looking down. "It was a good thing they found you when they did," she said. "The tide might have come back up and washed you away."

I woke up with a nurse above me, looking down. "You didn't make it," she said. "Now close your eyes, go back to sleep."

Treetops bend their backs to the wind. Gravity loses its focus. Every morning I wake knowing my cells have been swapped with others.

Deep within the lake exists the inside of my head. I look up into the blue. Everything is a mirror. Some days I'm a frog. Some days I'm the lake. Some days I'm the blue.

Like every other brick, I am immovable.

The refrigerator hums. The clock is stalled. A faucet drips in steady rhythm.

~

Your toothbrush is gone and I swear I didn't touch it. I loved that toothbrush like it was my own, though I could never bring myself to use it, I couldn't even lift it if I tried. Your toothbrush was too heavy, like the sword in the stone, but in this case the toothbrush in the plastic cup. Your toothbrush was so heavy it exerted its own gravitational pull. Dust mites revolved around it. I know I did.

Every morning and every evening I brush my teeth. With the exception of breathing, I do nothing else with such regularity. Brushing my teeth is the first and last activity I perform each day. Some days I even brush a third time, mid-afternoon. Despite my best efforts, cavities form. My teeth are more sensitive than they used to be.

My toothbrush is more sensitive too. It slouches, head hung low. Late at night I hear my toothbrush crying, stifled sobs, like it's ashamed to be taking the loss so hard. But I don't judge. I know how it feels.

Where your toothbrush once stood, now stands a complete lack-of-your-toothbrush, and this negative space seems heavier than your toothbrush ever did. It exerts its own gravity, but nothing revolves around this absence. It's a black hole, sucking everything in, like a drainpipe for the universe, and your toothbrush, the only plug that will fit.

~

It had been over twenty years since I'd seen him. We were just kids back then. I was a grade ahead. I hadn't seen or heard from him since I went off to high school. We shook hands. His grip was so firm I realized this man could easily strangle me. If it came down to me or him, I wouldn't stand a chance. He smiled and said, "Hey, how are ya?"

"Good," I said, squeezing back weakly. "It's great to see you." I had to tilt my head upward to look into his eyes.

He looked down and asked, "What's new?"

I didn't know what to say. Most of my life had happened since I'd last seen him. Every cell in my body had been replaced. I was a completely different person. "Not much," I said. "What about you?"

"Oh, it's pretty much the same," he said.

Except now we were men, or at least he was. Standing next to him I felt like a child. If you gave him a knife and a box of matches, he'd survive the worst of it. Me? I'd be building a cabin out of toothpicks.

I didn't even remember his name. He was the one to approach me in line at the grocery store, my cart overflowing. He had a bag of rice, a bag of dried lentils, and a bottle of multivitamins. Somehow it would be enough. I looked over my cart. It wouldn't sustain me for a week.

"Been in town long?" I asked.

"Never left," he said.

"Neither did I," I said, imagining our lives, seen from above. We'd gone decades without bumping into one another. Our lives, perfectly unsynchronized. I stepped onto the front of the bus as he departed through the back. I chose a lottery ticket while he passed the convenience store window. We'd seen the same movies, sat in the same seat, but on different nights. Our lives had intersected, but the timing was always off. It didn't seem possible.

"You okay?" he said.

"Oh, sure," I said, "just hard to believe it's been so long."

"Tell me about it."

But I didn't know what else say. Not sure what to ask. At this point he was a total stranger. I didn't know who he was, or what he was capable of, though it seemed he'd be capable of just about anything. I prayed that no one had given him a knife and a box of matches. I prayed that it hadn't come to that yet.

The cashier rang up my total. I paid and said, "Well, it was great to see you. We should try to catch up sometime."

He smiled and said, "I'd like that."

But we both knew it would never happen, and if I was lucky enough, our lives would never brush up against one another again.

~

The lake is black ink. The moon, nearly full, dominates the sky. Few stars can outshine it. The lake's surface glimmers. Crickets and frogs undertone the silence. A soft breeze swishes through distant trees, a boat tugs against its mooring. The constant lap of waves lulls the night toward sleep, where it teeters on the verge.

A long moment passes. Minutes or hours. Finally, a loon wails in the dark. It wails again and again, and yet, no response.

The branches rest, the wind momentarily immobile. Goose honks congregate in the distance. The horizon hums, as if in deep thought. A thin veil of cloud resides just above it. A loon warbles. The lake glints. The moon lounges. A star winks.

Then the breeze turns up the volume of the trees. The chorus of frogs and lapping waves plays on repeat. A fish breaks the surface. A cloud gathers round the moon, but its soft underbelly lets the pale light seep through. The horizon stretches to its limit. A loon whoops, but takes its time. The night still teeters on the edge, like it might last all night.

~

The building climbs higher into the sky, floor by innumerable floor. At this rate it takes years to ascend the flights of stairs, and by the time you reach the top, it'll have climbed that much higher, it would be like starting again. It's the way this city works: one day you're on top, the next you're a dust mite, which isn't so bad, it just takes some getting used to.

First the brain must ignite. Then the heart must beat. The sun pokes it head through a hole in a cloud and focuses a narrow tunnel of light onto the city. A pigeon perched on a steeple looks up, cleansed of all sin. I'm feeling lighter than ever before. My shoes no longer grip the pavement.

I remember hiding in the forest, peeking out from the undergrowth, when the lights in my house turned on. I remember a phone ringing, my eyes brimming. I remember the city popped up overnight. I was hiding in the forest as, one by one, the buildings sprouted from the earth.

Take it one step at a time, no need to rush, no need to say a thing, let your feet speak for you. The pigeon's heart beats gracefully, its soul washed and hung out to dry. I'm three feet from the ground. I need an anchor. Did you realize that every night the streets swap their signs in some elaborate prank? I thought I was finally getting a grip, but it's completely slipped. Can you pass me something to hold on to?

A hammer slams a bolt into place. A wrench tightens the nut. The walls are poured, the concrete hardens, the next floor is begun. For every step you take, another is added and the staircase spirals closer to infinity. I'm getting dizzy just thinking about it.

I was in bed with my back to the wall, feeling like I was on the other side of the wall, in my bed, my back to the wall. I remember reaching beneath my pillow—I'd left something there, a tooth or a note, or a telephone. The voice said, "Sorry, wrong number." Oddly, the voice was yours, but you were rounding a corner, climbing the next flight of stairs. I remember my eyes brimming. The pigeon takes off now, suffused with light. I'm out of reach, and drifting. The city sprawls. The building reaches higher. There's no stopping it now. One day soon you'll step from the roof onto the moon and peer down at us all. If you're waiting for me, please wait a little longer. If you give up, I will too. If the phone rings, pick it up. It might just be a wrong number at the right time.

~

Just then, the phone rang. I picked up the receiver and said, "Hello?"

"How are you feeling?"

"I already answered this question. What's the next one?"

"There is no next one," the voice said. "This is it."

"I feel a butterfly in my heart. Like the tide controlled solely by the moon. I feel like the rain will start at any second. I feel the windowpane against my palm. I feel cold. I feel that the world awaits. That the doorknobs aren't broken—"

"Thank you. Your results have been recorded. Please don't leave town. You won't make it far."

The line went dead, and I placed the receiver in its cradle. I stilled the butterfly in my heart and the rising tide inside me. Then I picked up my umbrella and placed my hand on the doorknob.

~

Last but not least, you boarded the train and sat down in a window seat. You looked out at the station platform and smiled. Even from this distance your eyes were tiny lakes that mirrored whatever they saw, and what they saw was me, standing on a shoreline, waving goodbye while you drifted away in your red canoe. Waves drawing you further and further. I didn't expect to take a second look, but I did: your train long gone for years.

●●●

All night the city unfolds like a map of the city. Its streets are named, its avenues numbered. Its houses are given a place to live. Parks, like tiny green islands, emerge throughout the concrete ocean. Swing sets swing in the breeze. Slides spiral upward in the moonlight. Monkey bars climb into position. Telephone poles line the sidewalks, and pigeons settle on their wires. Below the surface, the subway train tunnels along like a giant mole, blind but purposeful, poking its nose up at every station. And back on the street, the traffic light blinks, hoping to attract a car or a truck, the way the other lights attract moths.

~

Earlier I said most days I'm completely anonymous. I didn't mention it then, but some nights I'm also invisible. Well, that's not exactly true. More like I'm camouflaged. People see me but don't register that I'm actually there.

Last night I walked into a local bar, a small, intimate place. Low ceilings, a few occupied tables, and a few stools at the bar, which were all taken as well. I leaned up against an exposed limestone wall and listened to a young woman playing guitar and singing "The Sound of Silence."

The waitress passed by, carrying a tray of pints and wineglasses. I pressed myself closer to the wall to keep out of her way, but when she returned, she didn't stop to take my order. She wasn't ignoring me, she just hadn't seen me.

My shirt was grey, my pants were grey, my arms and legs and hands were grey. The truth is that I stood against the wall and not a single person knew I was there. I felt like the ghost of myself. It was entirely isolating but also strangely comforting. I could drift in like a gust of cool air, and no one would even look up, and I could drift out again undetected.

But the longer I stood there, the more I seemed to fade. I could see right through my hands. My shoes were already gone. The girl onstage was singing for me, my ghost, for my heart, deep as a well of silence, but equally as dark and mysterious. The waitress continued to pass me, bright smile flashing. I turned and slipped out through a crack in the door. The night outside was cold and damp.

Walking alone in the empty streets, I felt like a restless dream, a ghost in a sheet. Beneath a street light I paused and turned my head back toward the bar, where the sound of applause rose and subsided, then I drifted on.

~

When you left, it was up to me to let everyone know. I had to tell my parents, my co-workers, the phone company, neighbours, strangers, everyone. Gone. That's what I told them. Anywhere but here. I said that too. Everywhere but here. That's what I meant.

When you left, I stared at the phone. I put my hand on the receiver, but it was too heavy, or I was too weak, it wouldn't budge—for the best, because my voice had left too.

An envelope on the table. A hospital bed. A train departing the station. A frantic search of the streets. A faded poster stapled to a telephone pole. A long-distance phone call. Your name printed in the local paper. A postcard from another world. A goodbye that isn't a goodbye because maybe I'll see you again. A goodbye that's goodbye because maybe I won't.

When I finally picked up the phone, you were the first person I thought to call. I dialled your number. You picked up and said, "Hello?"

"You're gone," I said. "You shouldn't be answering the phone."

"I didn't," you said.

I looked down at the phone. The receiver was resting in its cradle, heavier than ever, and I felt weak.

Mostly there was silence. When I said you were gone, no one knew what to say. I didn't know what to say either. So even the shortest silence lasted forever. Eventually someone spoke, but the silence lingered beneath the words. It's still there, if you listen close enough.

"Hang up," I said.

"You first," you replied.

Gone. That's what I told them. That's what you told me by not saying a thing. Anywhere but here. Everywhere I'm not. Looking down at the phone, still in its cradle. Wondering how to turn thought into words. My throat full of stones. I swallowed them. Then I picked up the phone.

"No, you didn't," you said.

~

It was late when I finally returned home from my walk. The whole neighbourhood was asleep. A lone cat crossed the street, but otherwise the night was still, the moon pinned to the sky's black lapel, a few slumberous stars peering down.

I'd walked my normal route along the lake, but I'd taken my time. And in that time I'd become an old man. My teeth were about to slip out of my mouth, I needed a cane and suspenders, and I should have been sitting in a rocking chair with a troop of children gathered around my feet. I'd tell them this:

That night, as I returned from my walk, I noticed something on the roof of my house. From the end of the street, it was just a dark lump above my front door. I was directly below it before I could tell it was a pigeon hunched on the eaves trough. Its eyes were open. Its beak turned down in a grimace.

There was something mildly ominous about the situation. If it had been a raven or a crow, I might have considered it a harbinger of death, but a pigeon? What could that mean? Part of me wanted to get a broom and scare it off, but another part thought, "Regardless of what the pigeon symbolizes, it's still just a pigeon, resting after a long day of seeking crumbs."

I left the pigeon alone. It wasn't my place to disturb the bird, ominous or not. I unlocked my door and stepped inside. It was late and there wasn't much else for me to do, so I washed my face, brushed my teeth, climbed into bed.

My joints ached and my hip was giving me grief. My hair fell out strand by strand. My skin felt thin, though deeply wrinkled. I was my grandfather. Light as a feather. Withered.

The next morning I was back to my old self, which, in fact, was my younger self. I felt strange though, like I was *too* young, much younger than the day before. I wondered about my grandfather. If I was this young, maybe he was still alive. I could sit by his feet while he sat in his rocking chair, telling me a story from his childhood.

The prairie stretched out forever in every direction. He stood in the centre of it all, watching a flock of tiny black birds fill the sky. There were thousands, flying as one. Expanding, contracting, and never once did any two collide.

~

A black fly lands on my face. I brush it away, but it follows close behind.

Here, in the wilderness, I am in the fly's domain. I'm unprepared for what lies ahead. I search my pockets: a few receipts, clumps of lint, a lone dime. The fly swirls around my head like a frantic thought.

How long can a person last without food or water or sleep or fresh air or love or a kind touch or the will keep on going? I keep on going though I have no idea where I'm headed. The fly is my only company. My dearest friend, my one true love. Now when it lands on my face I let it linger. The days pass slowly with no one else to talk to. "How long have we been out here?" I ask.

I keep walking, and the trees keep parting before me. "It feels like weeks, like the world has whimpered away, and now it's just us, do you feel that too?" The fly walks across my cheek, rests beside my left nostril. "It wouldn't be so bad, we've got each other, and that's what really matters."

The trees open and I'm standing on the shoreline of a vast body of water. A red canoe floats on the waves. "I've been here before, in this life, or some other..." I'm in need of direction now, a sign nailed to a tree, or a sign from the sky above. The fly wanders along my face, searching for a sign of its own.

"It would be easier if I was hopelessly lost, if I could never make it home, but I know that if I turned around and walked back the way I came, I'd wind up at my front door. Eventually I'll have to go back. This place isn't meant for me, I wouldn't last a day." The fly has discovered the corner of my eye. "And my world, it's not meant for you. No one would understand us, we'd be torn apart in a matter of minutes."

The fly sucks up a small droplet of sweat, or a tear from its duct, it feels like a gentle kiss. Then it sets its wings into motion, lifts from my face. At first it circles tightly around my head, but its arcs grow larger and larger. When it reaches the furthest limits of its elliptic orbit and I can hardly hear its buzz, I cry out, "Don't leave me, please." I reach for the fly, grasp at the air wildly, but it's too late. "I'm not ready for you to go yet. I'm not ready to say goodbye." I'm at the edge of the lake, waves sweeping toward my feet, and the red canoe has disappeared, replaced by a solitary loon, staring at me with its red eyes.

•••

A curious automobile creeps up to an intersection. It pauses, scanning the streets for danger. Minutes pass before it drops its guard and beckons others to join. An old pickup approaches. Then a blue minivan. Then a bus followed by a taxi, followed by a taxi, followed by a garbage truck, followed by a taxi... The traffic builds. It slows to stop-and-go. Tensions mount. A red convertible speeds through a red light—the screech of brakes, the squeal of tires—and slams into a black SUV. The sickening crunch of impact. Smoke rises from their hoods. Alarms cry out, horns blare, and the city wonders if it will ever sleep again.

~

I've put this off far too long, but here it goes: Hello, it's lovely to meet you. My name is I don't know. I never needed one. Until now, that is. That's right. Until now, that is. I don't know. I put it off too long.

Hello, it's been too long. I waited at the edge of the cemetery, but you never showed. I shook hands with the leafless oak. Its name was it didn't know. It never needed one. Until then, that is. That's wrong. Until then, that is. It didn't know. A crow looked down and cocked its head to one side.

It's an odd question to ask, but do you have a spare battery? The clock's hands are stuck in place, and we're trapped in that space between tick and tock, like a moment stalled in forever, or a grain of sand falling through an hourglass the size of the universe.

The universe expands, we shrink. Our hands reach across the void and clasp one another. Hello, I thought I'd never see you again. I need to rub the sand from my eyes. When they open, you're already gone. Hello?

Better safe than sorry. I'm so sorry. I don't know if I ever told you that. The tree stood in the rain, its naked limbs dripping. The crow hung its head lower. The lake watched from a respectful distance.

Until then, that's all I remember. After that it's, Hello, my name is I still don't know. To be honest, I don't really want one. I'm fearful of that level of commitment. I put it off too long. Then I put it off longer.

On the other side of forgetting, you wait for me to arrive. I said I'd be there soon, but something came up. You're not going to believe it. I stick out my hand and say, "Hello, it's lovely to meet you. Did you bring the battery, like I asked?"

~

What would happen if I closed my eyes? Would everything stay still or would I wind up someplace new, someplace entirely unfounded? I'm serious. I often wake in the most bizarre locations—a train platform, among horses in a barn, on a sandy shoreline, waves crashing beside me, inside a cardboard box with holes punched in the lid... Once I woke on the edge of a city floating above the lake, the moon reflected in its still mirror. I looked up. The sky was endless, the stars infinite. One had been named after you, but I couldn't tell which.

~

In the cemetery a steady rain settled in. Nothing else needed to be said, but the hole had yet to be filled. I placed my hand on the headstone. It was heavy and cold, and your name had been etched into it forever. Car doors closed and engines turned over and I was last to leave. I looked down at my feet. A shoelace had come undone.

My parents' car idled. I opened the door and climbed inside. As we pulled away, I looked out to where we'd left you, soaking in the hereafter.

The other cars were gone, and we drove slowly down the lane. Dad in the driver's seat, Mom in the passenger's. The radio was off. No one spoke. The rain pattering on the roof said it all. We passed through the rows, down the slope toward the gate, and turned onto the road. The rain poured down now. The wipers couldn't keep up. The world appeared under water. No one continued to speak as we drove home, taking the scenic route, along the bottom of the lake.

~

Just then, the phone rang. I picked up the receiver and said, "Hello?"

"Hello, Mr. Macintosh."

"You've got the wrong number," I said. "I've been through this before."

"This is the number I have on file."

"Then you need to update your files."

"That is precisely what I am doing, sir. Can I put you on a brief hold? It'll only take a minute." And before I could say a word, a crackly fifties tune played in my ear. I waited. I waited for ten minutes. Waited and listened and tapped my foot and understood none of it. Suddenly the music cut out and they were back, though their voice was winded, as if they'd been running for their life.

"Hello? Mr. Macintosh?" the voice rushed out. "We're having a problem with your request—" the voice gasped, it sounded desperate.

"What's going on over there? Are you okay?" Down the line I heard a crash and rumble, like a building collapsing. "Hello?" I continued. "Are you still there?"

"Oh yes, still here." The voice was strained. "We...we're, we're having technical problems—" A fit of coughing erupted, wet and throaty, and weaker with each cough. "We're having problems with your request." Again, the voice broke into a cough.

"That's okay," I said. "Please, don't worry about me. You've got to get some help."

"I fear you may be right," the voice choked out, "but there's no help out there, only darkness, and it's growing darker every day."

"You've got to get out," I pleaded, "you've got to save yourself."

"There's no being saved for someone like me..." The voice hushed. The line crackled in the silence. A moment later the voice said, "I'm going soon, will you wait with me?"

"Tell me where you are, I'll call someone."

"Please...don't hang up. I don't think I can do this alone..."

"I'm here," I said. "I'm not going anywhere."

"Thank you." The voice went quiet, coughed softly. "I really am sorry," it croaked, "about your request..."

"You did the best you could," I said. "You did everything. And more."

"Really?" The voice brightened, so light it was nearly gone. "Everything and more... Yes, that's right. Everything and more..."

There was a clunk, then the crackle of static.

I sat there motionless, uncertain of what to do next. I couldn't hang up the phone. It didn't feel right. So I set down the receiver, slid on my shoes, and headed out the door, nearly stepping on another dead bird abandoned on my welcome mat.

~

A chill crept into the air and the backyard was littered with leaves. Every gust brought down more. The sun was shifting south, the days losing hours. The sky was a brilliant blue upon which a few stray clouds conveyed their thoughts. Deep within each, snowflakes were gestating, not yet ready to be born. From a high branch, a black squirrel chattered at me in annoyance, as if I were the cause of this sudden shift in degrees.

•••

The city, ever sprawling, bumps into the lake. The lake waves hello, goodbye, hello, goodbye... The city doesn't know where else to go. When it continues forward, its bricks just sink. The lake ripples in delight. The city steps back into itself and stacks its bricks. The lake retreats, gathers its waves, and surges forward, but breaks against a wall the city has erected to keep the water out. The lake waits patiently. It knows everything will come to it in time.

~

The staff party wouldn't end. Management hadn't shown up. Maybe there was more than rum in the punch. Things were getting out of control.

John was babbling about the coming rapture—the world on fire and then underwater. He'd grow loud, like he was preaching from a mountaintop, then quiet to a whisper, like it was a secret only we were lucky enough to know.

Omar stayed glued to the television set, working through the box of VHS tapes he'd found in storage. Occasionally he'd burst into laughter or sobs or horrified gasps. When one tape finished, he ejected it and inserted another: security camera footage of a staff party in a conference room, this conference room, this party, we were all there. I saw myself on the screen, turning to look up at the camera in the corner of the room, so I turned and looked up at the camera in the corner of the room.

"Can you put on something else?" I asked.

"This is all we've got," he said. "It's gripping. I can't wait to see what happens next."

I saw myself walking away, so I walked away.

Margery was still seated at her desk, knitting a scarf. "This scarf will wrap around the equator," she said without looking up, "to keep it warm, when the next ice age hits."

"You've been at it for centuries, haven't you?" I asked.

"I started it when the party started," she said. "I hope to have it finished by the time everyone leaves."

The scarf had grown considerably in the time we chatted; it piled on the floor around her, up to her knees. I'd have thought her hands would be a blur, but they worked slowly, thoughtfully, like she had all the time in the world.

Yoko sat on the floor in the centre of her office. Back straight, legs folded tightly beneath her, hands resting on her knees. She breathed deeply, spoke in long, measured words...

"Time. Form. Breath. Stardust. Time. Form. Breath..." It was hypnotic, a mantra, a prayer. Her hands moved now, though her eyes remained closed. She pulled a red gas canister from behind her back, lifted and poured it over her head, still chanting, "Stardust. Time. Form..." She reached into her pocket, retrieved a book of matches, and tore one loose. She struck the match and dropped it into her lap. Her body was engulfed in one huge flame. It filled her office with bright, unrelenting heat. The fire alarm remained silent, the sprinklers dry. I had to back out of her office and close the door. Even then I could still hear, "Breath. Stardust. Time..."

Back in the conference room, Nadia was claustrophobic and panicking: "This party has been going on for years..." Her eyes were strained, bloodshot. "Why haven't any of you noticed?" She was desperate, nearly foaming at the mouth. "My children are going to be grown up and moved away by the time I get home. I'm missing my life. We all are..." She shook Jim by the collar. "Why don't you wake up to the fact that outside this building the entire world has moved on? We're forgotten to them. We're nothing but ghosts."

But Jim just cracked a smile and said, "Are there any chips left? I've got a craving for some plain chips, ruffled, if we've got them."

~

I was late. As usual I was late. But never this late. The subway train was quiet and I was alone. I tried to look out the window, but only glimpsed my reflection staring back. My breath fogged the glass.

The train slowed as we approached a station. I looked up when the doors opened. My mother stepped inside, and the doors hissed close behind her.

I grabbed a handrail and stood, my legs shaking. "Mom?" I choked out. "After all this time. Is that you?"

The train started forward and she stumbled a little. "I'm sorry. You must be mistaken." Her voice hadn't changed in all these years.

"I know it's been a while, but you couldn't have forgotten me."

"I'm sorry. I don't believe we've ever met."

"I wasn't running away from you. I was running from myself. Searching for something I never found. But now you've found me."

My mother stepped back.

"I tried to find my way home," I told her, "but I was lost. When I finally made it back, the house was gone. This city had taken its place."

She stared at me.

"It's me, Mom. I'm here."

"It's impossible," she said, more to herself than to me. She shook her head and looked away.

The train slowed to a stop, and the doors opened. My mother stepped through without even saying goodbye. The doors closed, and suddenly she turned, her cheeks wet, eyes wide with realization, and her hand reaching while the train pulled me away.

The dark subway tunnel rushed past, but I couldn't see it, just my own pale reflection. The lights flickered. I looked up. It was almost my stop. And about time too. I couldn't believe the hour. I leaned my head against the coolness of the window. My breath fogged the glass.

~

I was brushing my teeth and getting ready for bed when I realized I hadn't called you. Today of all days. I expected your call by now. I waited by the phone, but it never rang. I held the receiver in my hand, but couldn't remember your number.

I spoke to the operator, said, "Can you connect me to my sadness?" But the operator said, "You already are." You of all people should know what today is. The day I forgot to call. The day I remembered, but it was too late. The day after yesterday, right?

I wrote down your number, but the numbers were all wrong. I couldn't get a dial tone. I didn't have a quarter, and anyways, payphones cost two now. I dialled, but so slowly that the day passed before I could finish. It was foggy and I couldn't see the numbers. I couldn't find the phone among the stacks of boxes. Then the phone started ringing; the receiver was in my hand.

"Hello?" you said.

"Hello, Blue," I replied.

The phone was ringing. I picked up the receiver, said, "Hello?" and your voice replied, "Hello, Blue."

The phone was ringing. I was dialling the sky, and the birds on the telephone line scattered.

It was too late, you'd been gone too long. I should have called earlier. You were waiting for your phone to ring, and when you answered, I said, "I'm sorry I forgot to call."

It was too late, I'd been gone too long. I didn't have reception, and even if I did, my phone bills were past due, my account suspended. Your voice said, "I'm sorry I didn't answer the phone." The phone was ringing. The blue phone.

Today of all days. You of all people. The caller ID displayed: UNKNOWN NAME UNKNOWN NUMBER. It could have been anyone. It could have been you, or it could have been me, though likely not, because it was too late by the time I remembered.

The phone rings and rings and rings. Today. Yesterday. Three days from now. I couldn't get through. You always called, so I was worried. I hadn't heard from you in years, but today of all days...

Look at this phone. It's waited centuries to ring. The ringing never stops, even when you pick up. I picked up. You picked up.

A voice said, "Goodbye, Blue."

~

I woke in the night, my stomach growling like a portly raccoon. I shuffled downstairs to the kitchen, opened the refrigerator door, and saw my grandfather out there on the snow-swept prairie. He was far away and walking in the wrong direction. I called to him. Again and again I called to him, but he couldn't hear me for the wind. When I tried to step inside, the chill took my breath away. I wasn't dressed for rescue, standing in the kitchen at midnight in my housecoat and slippers. I held on to the door and called uselessly while Grandpa, driven by confusion or determination, wandered further into the blizzard and was soon erased. I lifted the milk from the shelf and closed the door. I poured a glass and drank it slowly. When I opened the door again, the blizzard raged on. I knew Grandpa was gone, he wouldn't be coming back. I closed the door and shuffled back upstairs, climbed into bed, and pulled the covers up to my neck, doing what I could to drive away the chill.

~

I stood at the train station, waiting, as always. An old steam engine pulled in with a loud groan. A car door opened and you stepped out. I could hardly breathe through the lump in my throat. As the train pulled away, we wrapped our arms around each other. I was on the verge of tears.

After all this time there was so much to say, I'd rehearsed for years, the words welling inside me, but I forgot where to start. An old engine pulled in behind you, releasing a loud hiss of steam that tousled your hair around your face.

A strand of hair lay across your cheek. I brushed it away. "This is my train," you said. "I can't miss it."

I looked in your eyes, knowing you were right. This was your train, you couldn't miss it.

You turned and stepped onto the train. No. That's not right.

A strand of hair lay across your cheek. I brushed it away. "This your train," you said, "you can't miss it."

I looked in your eyes, knowing you were right. This was my train, I couldn't miss it. My throat was too tight, I couldn't speak. I squeezed you once more, and you released me. My feet started, and I followed them onto the train and down the aisle. Every seat was occupied by me—a younger me, an older me, a ghostly me, a woman me, a you me...

I selected the last vacant seat and sat down, pressed my hand to the window. With one loud wail, the train hauled me toward the present, and you stood alone at the station, waiting, as always.

•••

The city doesn't sleep as often as it should, but some nights, when cars are tucked into their garages and pigeons huddle on a wire, when picnic tables doze like horses, when the streets are thankful for their many nightlights, when a black cat slinks into its shadow, when skyscrapers stop to catch their breath, when flags rest against their poles, and the moths have finally settled, the city sighs and sinks into a slumber so deep it dreams of breaking away from the ground and lifting into the air, like a giant concrete iceberg. Slowly it rises into the sky. A steady breeze drifts it over the lake. Far below, someone stands on the shoreline, looking up. The city has no idea who it is, or how they were left behind.

Acknowledgements

Stuart Ross sparked the writing of this novel during a phone conversation in 2018; he also brought that conversation full circle with his insightful edits, his boundless encouragement, and by publishing this book through 1366. Nicholas Papaxanthos read and offered direction on an early draft. The Ontario Arts Council afforded extra hours and headspace to write and edit the manuscript. Fidel Peña knocked my socks off with his cover design. Michael Mirolla and all the folks at Guernica Editions made these words physical. My parents gave me lungs, among everything else. Allison, Etta, and Jonas fill my life with life. My lake-deep gratitude to all.

Also by Michael e. Casteels

A Sudden Change of Season (Proper Tales Press, 2024)

ONDO (nOIR:Z, 2022)

The Man with the Spider Scar (Puddles of Sky Press, 2021)

All We've Learned, Which Isn't Much (w/ Nicholas Papaxanthos,
    above/ground press, 2020)

Flotsam (Timglaset, 2020)

& Jetsam (Simulacrum Press, 2019)

Words I Never Said (No press, 2019)

The Last White House at the End of the Row of White Houses (Invisible, 2016)

solar-powered light bulb & the lake's achy tooth (Apt 9. Press, 2015)

3 chapters toward an epic (phafours, 2014)

Michael e. Casteels is a writer, musician, collage artist, outdoor enthusiast, and part-time stay-at-home dad. He is also co-curator of the Arbitrary Islands Island Archive, a library on Lumpy Denommee's Island. His work has appeared in small press publications across Canada and internationally, most recently the collage Westerns *ONDO* (nOIR:Z, 2022) and *The Man with the Spider Scar* (Puddles of Sky Press, 2021). His first collection of poetry, *The Last White House at the End of the Row of White Houses*, was published by Invisible Publishing in 2016. He is the editor, designer, and bookmaker at Puddles of Sky Press in Kingston.

About 1366 Books

1366 Books is an imprint of Guernica Editions, launched in 2024 to bring to light two books of innovative but accessible fiction annually. Each title—whether a novel, stories, or microfictions—is a unique literary experience. Imprint editor Stuart Ross welcomes submissions of fiction manuscripts that challenge or attempt to redefine the boundaries of the genre. He is especially interested in seeing manuscripts of experimental fiction from members of diverse and marginalized communities. Write to Stuart at 1366books@gmail.com.

2024
The Apple in the Orchard, by Brian Dedora
Strange Water, by Sarah Moses

2025
Furthermore, the Lake, by Michael e. Casteels

Exploding Fictions

MIX
Paper
FSC® C100212
FSC
www.fsc.org

Printed by Imprimerie Gauvin
Gatineau, Québec